koala

This book belongs to

....

frog comes down

splash!

pig is **clean**

oink

where's my mud?

grunt

pig is **dirty**

dog is **sad**

snail is slow

wait for me!

shark is fast

must dash!

zoooom!

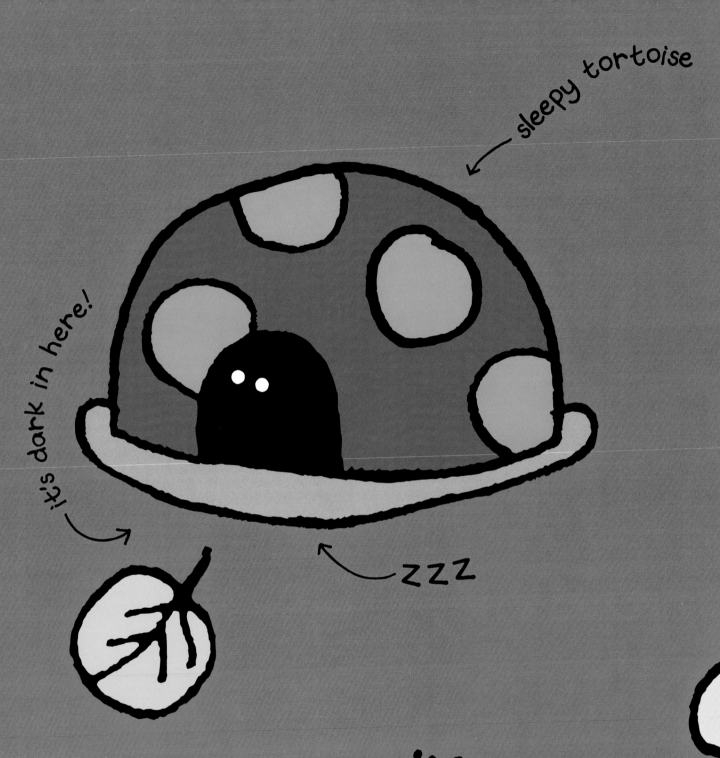

sleepy tortoise

it's dark in here!

zzz

tortoise is **in**

tortoise comes out

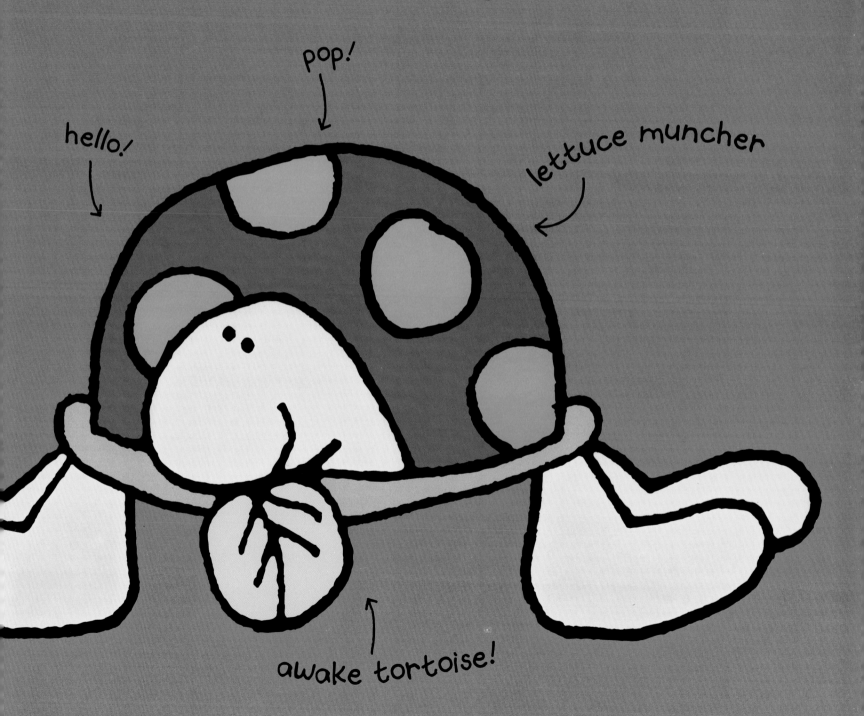

pop!

hello!

lettuce muncher

awake tortoise!

fish is tiny

splish

I wish I were as huge as a whale

splash

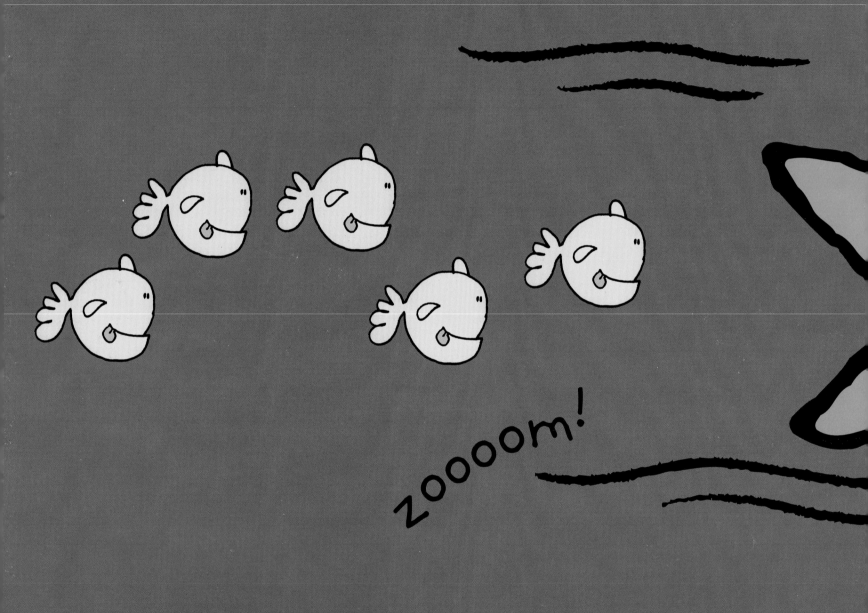

byeeeeee

bang on the door ™ ©

OXFORD
UNIVERSITY PRESS

Great Clarendon Street, Oxford OX2 6DP

Oxford   New York

Auckland Bangkok Buenos Aires Cape Town Chennai Dar es Salaam Delhi Hong Kong
Istanbul Karachi Kolkata Kuala Lumpur Madrid Melbourne Mexico City Mumbai
Nairobi São Paulo Shanghai Taipei Tokyo Toronto

Oxford is a registered trade mark of Oxford University Press
in the UK and in certain other countries

Text © Oxford University Press 2003

www.bangonthedoor.com

The moral rights of the author and artists have been asserted

Database right Oxford University Press (maker)

First published 2003

British Library Cataloguing in Publication Data available

ISBN 0-19-272566-1

1 3 5 7 9 10 8 6 4 2

Typeset in Freeflow

Printed in China